Women in Chemistry

Major Women in Science

Women in Chemistry

Kim Etingoff

Mason Crest

Mason Crest
450 Parkway Drive, Suite D
Broomall, Pennsylvania 19008
www.masoncrest.com

Printed and bound in the United States of America.

First printing
9 8 7 6 5 4 3 2 1

Series ISBN: 978-1-4222-2923-1
ISBN: 978-1-4222-2925-5
ebook ISBN: 978-1-4222-8894-8

The Library of Congress has cataloged the
        hardcopy format(s) as follows:

Library of Congress Cataloging-in-Publication Data

Etingoff, Kim.
  Women in chemistry / Kim Etingoff.
      pages cm. -- (Major women in science)
  Audience: Grade 7 to 8.
  Includes bibliographical references and index.
   ISBN 978-1-4222-2925-5 (hardcover) -- ISBN 978-1-4222-2923-1 (series) -- ISBN 978-1-4222-8894-8 (ebook)
  1. Women chemists--Biography--Juvenile literature. 2. Chemistry--Vocational guidance--Juvenile literature. I. Title.
  QD21.E85 2014
  540.92'52--dc23
                        2013009817

Produced by Vestal Creative Services.
www.vestalcreative.com

Contents

Introduction

Have you wondered about how the natural world works? Are you curious about how science could help sick people get better? Do you want to learn more about our planet and universe? Are you excited to use technology to learn and share ideas? Do you want to build something new?

Scientists, engineers, and doctors are among the many types of people who think deeply about science and nature, who often have new ideas on how to improve life in our world.

We live in a remarkable time in human history. The level of understanding and rate of progress in science and technology have never been greater. Major advances in these areas include the following:

- Computer scientists and engineers are building mobile and Internet technology to help people access and share information at incredible speeds.
- Biologists and chemists are creating medicines that can target and get rid of harmful cancer cells in the body.
- Engineers are guiding robots on Mars to explore the history of water on that planet.
- Physicists are using math and experiments to estimate the age of the universe to be greater than 13 billion years old.
- Scientists and engineers are building hybrid cars that can be better for our environment.

Scientists are interested in discovering and understanding key principles in nature, including biological, chemical, mathematical, and physical aspects of our world. Scientists observe, measure, and experiment in a systematic way in order to test and improve their understanding. Engineers focus on applying scientific knowledge and math to find creative solutions for technical problems and to develop real products for people to use. There are many types of engineering, including computer, electrical, mechanical, civil, chemical, and biomedical engineering. Some people have also found that studying science or engineering can help them succeed in other professions such as law, business, and medicine.

Both women and men can be successful in science and engineering. This book series highlights women leaders who have made significant contributions across many scientific fields, including chemistry, medicine, anthropology, engineering, and physics. Historically, women have faced barriers to training and building careers in science,

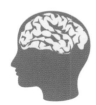

which makes some of these stories even more amazing. While not all barriers have been overcome, our society has made tremendous progress in educating and advancing women in science. Today, there are schools, organizations, and resources to enable women to pursue careers as scientists or engineers at the highest levels of achievement and leadership.

The goals of this series are to help you:

1. Learn about women scientists, engineers, doctors, and inventors who have made a major impact in science and our society
2. Understand different types of science and engineering
3. Explore science and math in school and real life

You can do a lot of things to learn more about science, math, and engineering. Explore topics in books or online, take a class at school, go to science camp, or do experiments at home. More important, talk to a real scientist! Call or e-mail your local college to find students and professors. They would love to meet with you. Ask your doctors about their education and training. Or you can check out these helpful resources:

- *Nova* has very cool videos about science, including profiles on real-life women scientists and engineers: www.pbs.org/wgbh/nova.
- *National Geographic* has excellent photos and stories to inspire people to care about the planet: science.nationalgeographic.com/science.
- Here are examples of online courses for students, of which many are free to use:
  1. Massachusetts Institute of Technology (MIT) OpenCourseWare highlights for high school: http://ocw.mit.edu/high-school
  2. Khan Academy tutorials and courses: www.khanacademy.org.
  3. Stanford University Online, featuring video courses and programs for middle and high school students: online.stanford.edu.

Other skills will become important as you get older. Build strong communication skills, such as asking questions and sharing your ideas in class. Ask for advice or help when needed from your teachers, mentors, tutors, or classmates. Be curious and resilient: learn from your successes and mistakes. The best scientists do.

Learning science and math is one of the most important things that you can do in school. Knowledge and experience in these areas will teach you how to think and how the world works and can provide you with many adventures and paths in life. I hope you will explore science—you could make a difference in this world.

Ann Lee-Karlon, PhD
President
Association for Women in Science
San Francisco, California

What Does It Take to Be a Chemist?

Many people know early on that they want to be scientists. They're curious about the world. They like asking questions and forming **hypotheses**. They might even conduct some experiments.

Lots of people think kids are natural scientists. They're curious about how the world works. And little girls are no exception.

By the time they're ready to choose a career, more and more women are choosing science. Some of those women, as well as plenty of men, are choosing chemistry. Chemistry is the study of matter—all the stuff the world is made out of. Chemists study tiny particles of matter and how they work together.

Some chemists study organic matter, which makes up living things. Others study matter that makes up nonliving things. And others study how matter changes and interacts with other matter. You can find women in all of these fields of chemistry.

A lot of people are attracted to careers in science. They have questions about the world they want to answer, and they find the **scientific method** to be a good way to think. They like coming up with questions about our world, then researching and possibly answering those questions. Careers in science just make sense for those people who tend to think scientifically.

In 2010, there were over 82,000 chemists in the United States. All of those people chose to get jobs in chemistry. Some work at universities. Others work for **pharmaceutical** companies, energy companies, or other businesses.

Choosing to Be a Chemist

Most young people have to take chemistry in high school. For some, it sparks their interest and holds it. Mixing chemicals to make reactions can be fun! A high school student might decide she wants to continue with chemistry. She's fascinated with all the discoveries chemistry allows her to make.

Some choose chemistry as a career because it's a way to help make the world a better place. People live better lives because of chemistry. Chemists discover new medicines. They research and come up with new sources of energy. They come up with ways to get rid of pollution. Lots of people want to make a difference in the world, and chemistry is one way to do that.

Education

It takes a long time to become a chemist. People who want to make chemistry a career have to go through several years of education before they reach their dream. After high school, there's a lot more education to go.

All chemists need at least a bachelor's degree, and usually an advanced degree. In undergraduate school, students who want a chemistry career will major in chemistry. They will take four years of chemistry courses, and will explore the

As a chemistry student, you will discover how our world works at the chemical level—while being trained for a rewarding career.

different kinds of chemistry. They'll move from basic chemistry courses to much more advanced ones. Other classes they might have to take include math, physics, English, and biology. They may even get to do research with professors, help publish papers, and write **theses**.

After undergraduate school, people who want to advance in chemistry go to graduate school. Generally, students go on to get their PhDs at a university. Chemists with PhDs have the best job options when they're done with school. Future chemists spend a lot of time in graduate school—five years or more. Usually the first year or two are made up of classes, and the rest of the time is spent in the lab. At the end of the PhD, students will have to defend a thesis.

By the time a student is in graduate school, she has picked a type of chemistry to focus on. She has figured out what she's most interested in researching. It could be solar energy . . . or pharmaceuticals . . . or magnets . . . or something

What Does It Take to Be a Chemist? 11

else. It's a big world, and chemistry has many, many applications! Now she will do a lot of research on that subject. She'll start to become an expert in the field she's chosen.

Some people are ready to become chemists at this point. They find work at a university or **company**. Others need a little more research experience first. Those people do post-doctoral studies. After getting their Ph.D., they spend a few more years doing research before they become a full chemist.

Character

Education is definitely an important part of being a chemist, but so is having the right character. Chemists must have certain qualities that help them be good scientists.

Chemists are usually pretty good at math. They think mathematically, and they enjoy using math to solve problems. If you like math, chemistry might be a good career choice for you. Computer skills are also useful, since lots of lab work actually involves computers.

Analytical skills are also important. Chemists carry out lots of experiments. They need to design them, run them, and then analyze them. It doesn't help much to run an experiment and get results if you can't figure out what they mean.

Patience is another great character trait for chemists to have. They need patience to run experiments that often take months or even years. Everything has to be very exact in an experiment, and it takes time to make sure that errors don't creep into the work.

Luckily, lots of people have these skills and want to be chemists. Women have been joining in the ranks of chemists in greater number during the last few decades, because they too have a passion for chemistry.

Words to Know

Hypotheses: educated guesses; possible explanations meant to explain facts, based on scientific evidence.

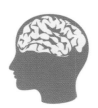

Scientific method: a procedural method followed by all scientists to answer questions about the world. The scientific method consists of observation, hypothesis, experimentation, and interpretation.

Pharmaceutical: related to medicinal drugs.

Theses: academic works that show results of original research, usually required for a master's or doctorate degree.

Company: a business owned by individuals and not run by the government.

Analytical skills: the ability to understand and solve complex problems.

Find Out More

Education Portal: Chemist
www.education-portal.com/articles/Chemist_Educational_Requirements_for_a_Career_in_Chemistry.html

U.S. Bureau of Labor Statistics,
"Occupational Outlook Handbook, Chemists and Materials Scientists"
www.bls.gov/ooh/life-physical-and-social-science/chemists-and-materials-scientists.htm#tab-1

2

Alice Hamilton:
Pioneer of Industrial Medicine

Imagine going to work every day for decades, only to find out later that your job was killing you. This was not unusual in the late nineteenth and early twentieth centuries—but it was not acceptable to Alice Hamilton.

Alice Hamilton was born on February 27, 1869, in Fort Wayne, Indiana. The Hamilton family was one of the city's founders. She had four sisters (one of them was author Edith Hamilton) and one brother. Alice was home-schooled for the first few years of her life, and then eventually graduated from Miss Porter's School, a boarding school in Connecticut. After graduation, Alice wanted to go to medical school; at the time, most medical schools accepted students with only a high-school education. But, like many all-girls schools, Miss Porter's did not offer its students many science courses. Alice spent the summer after high-school graduation studying chemistry and physics with a tutor, so she would be able to attend the University of Michigan Medical School in the fall.

As a student, Alice decided she was not interested in treating patients as a medical doctor. Instead, she was intrigued by pathology, the scientific study of the nature, origin, progress, and cause of disease. So, Alice decided to focus on a career in research.

Alice graduated from the University of Michigan Medical School in 1893. Following graduation, she completed internships at the Minneapolis Hospital for Women and Children and the New England Hospital for Women and Children. In 1895, Alice went to Europe to study bacteriology (the study of bacteria) and pathology. At that time, women were not welcome at many of the major universities in Germany. Her requests to work with Robert Koch, one of the founders of bacteriology, and Paul Ehrlich, a pioneer in immunology, were refused. She was, however, able to study at universities in Leipzig and Munich. When Alice returned to the United States in 1897, she enrolled in Johns Hopkins University Medical School, where she worked as a research assistant and continued her studies.

In 1897, Alice was offered, and accepted, a professorship in pathology at the Women's Hospital Medical College at Northwestern University in Chicago. When the college was closed in 1902, Alice accepted a position at the Memorial Institute for Infectious Diseases, where she then worked as a bacteriologist.

Not long after moving to Chicago, Alice heard a speech by social activist Jane Addams. Addams and Ellen Gates Starr had founded Hull House, a settlement house offering resources and support to the city's poor. Also living at Hull House were individuals—primarily women—who worked to fight the social problems of the day. After hearing Jane Addams speak, Alice decided she wanted to be one of those residents and moved into Hull House, where she lived for twenty-two years.

Alice learned a lot about working conditions while living in the settlement house. She wrote, "Life in a settlement does several things to you. Among others, it teaches you that education and culture have little to do with real wisdom, the wisdom that comes from life experiences." She met victims of industrial accidents; she heard stories about workers who got sick and died from exposure to carbon monoxide as they worked in steel mills; she learned of workers who had been disabled because of exposure to cyanide and arsenic as they worked. She also learned that, while there had been many studies on **industrial medicine**

in Europe, there had been no similar research conducted in the United States. She decided to use her knowledge of chemistry to investigate these problems in America.

In 1910, Illinois governor Charles Deneen appointed Alice to the new Occupational Diseases Commission. The first thing the commission had to do was create a list of dangerous occupations. Alice went from factory to factory, taking careful notes of the conditions faced by the workers, looking at air samples, and studying the dust covering the factory surfaces. Through her chemical research, the public was made aware of the dangers involved in many manufacturing processes.

Even before Alice's work with the Illinois commission was finished, the U.S. government contacted her about investigating factories all across the country. As a chemist, she was able to identify and understand the chemicals that were so dangerous to humans. Working for the Bureau of Labor, she spent many years investigating mines, mills, and smelters, learning all she could about the side effects suffered by the employees of those industries. She proposed regulations on ventilation, toxic risks, and other safeguards to protect workers. Her most influential studies concerned the dangers of lead and lead oxide, substances that were common in the paint industry.

Alice Hamilton has often been called the mother of occupational medicine. Her combination of social reform and knowledge of chemistry made her particularly effective. By 1919, she was considered the leading expert in industrial medicine. Harvard Medical School thought so highly of her abilities that it hired her as an assistant professor in the new Department of Industrial Medicine. Alice was the first female faculty member of the all-male Harvard University. But even though Alice broke the employment barrier at Harvard, she was not allowed to attend university social activities or participate in the graduation procession.

It was important to Alice that she continue her research, so she arranged to divide her time between her university responsibilities and her research. While at Harvard, Alice helped bring the hazards of dyes, carbon monoxide, mercury, radium, hydrogen sulfide gasses, and many more substances to the attention of the government, and to the public's attention as well. Chemistry allowed Alice to warn the world of the dangers of many industrial substances.

Alice became a valuable resource to health-related organizations. She served as the only female member of the League of Nations Health Committee from 1924 to 1930. In 1935, she served as a consultant on health issues to the U.S. Division of Labor Standards.

Her work brought Alice much recognition. In 1944, she was included on the list of Men in Science. In recognition of Alice's many years of work in industrial medicine, as well as her work on behalf of social issues, *Time* named her Woman of the Year in 1956. The U.S. Post Office issued a stamp in her honor in 1995. In 2002, the American Chemical Society placed a National Historical Chemical Landmark plaque at Hull House in Chicago, honoring Alice and her work in the development of occupational medicine.

What Else Did Alice Hamilton Do?

As prominent as Alice was in industrial medicine, this was not her only interest. Alice was an outspoken activist against World War I and one of the founders of the Woman's Peace Party. She was active in organizations such as the League of Women Voters, the National Consumer's League, and the American Civil Liberties Union. In 1927, she joined other high-profile individuals—such as Upton Sinclair, George Bernard Shaw, and H. G. Wells—in an attempt to prevent the execution of Nicola Sacco and Bartolomeo Vanzetti, who had been convicted of robbery and murder in a highly politicized trial. Their attempts failed, and the duo was executed on August 23, 1927. Alice also campaigned against McCarthyism, the 1953 execution of Julius and Ethel Rosenberg for espionage, and the Vietnam War. To find out more about these important events in history—events that Alice Hamilton influenced—look them up on the Internet or in the library!

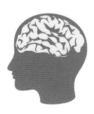

Alice lived a full and long life. She died in 1970, at age 101. She had used her knowledge of chemistry, her curiosity, and her passion to help others to truly change the world.

Words to Know

Industrial medicine: also called occupational medicine; the branch of medicine concerned with the treatment and prevention of diseases and injuries occurring in the workplace or caused by conditions there. Chemistry also plays a large role in industrial medicine.

Find Out More

Changing the Face of Medicine: Dr. Alice Hamilton.
www.nim.nih.gov/changingthefaceofmedicine/physicians/biography_137.html

Distinguished Women of Past and Present: Alice Hamilton.
www.distinguishedwomen.com/biographies/hamilton-a.html

Ginsberg, Judah, "Alice Hamilton and the Development of Occupational Medicine." American Chemical Society: National Historic Chemical Landmarks
acswebcontent.acs.org/landmarks/landmarks/hamilton/index.html

Hamilton, Alice. *Exploring the Dangerous Trades: The Autobiography of Alice Hamilton, M.D.* Denver, Colo.: Miller Press, 2008.

Sicherman, Barbara. *Alice Hamilton: A Life in Letters*. Champaign, Ill.: University of Illinois Press, 2003.

3

Maud Menten:
Researching Disease

Maud Menten's goal was to be a research scientist. All she wanted to do was help people, but she had to leave her country in order to do so.

Maud Leonora Menten was born March 20, 1879, in Port Lambton, Ontario. She was raised in the British Columbia countryside but returned to Ontario to attend the University of Toronto. She earned a Bachelor of Arts degree in natural science and English in 1904. In 1907, Maud received a master's degree in physiology (the study of living things and their body parts), also from the University of Toronto.

As Maud continued her medical studies, she was awarded a scholarship to the Rockefeller Institute for Medical Research in New York City. During 1907 and

1908, Maud studied the effect of radium bromide on tumors. She and two co-workers published the findings in the institute's first **monograph**. Maud enjoyed the research, and she proved to be quite good at it.

After completing her year at the Rockefeller Institute, and some additional time spent working as an intern at the Infirmary for Women and Children, Maud returned to Toronto to complete her medical degree. When she graduated in 1911, Maud became one of the first women in Canada to receive a doctorate in medicine. She stayed at the University of Toronto to work at Archibald Byron MacCallum's laboratory.

Maud's experience at the Rockefeller Institute had whetted her appetite for research. But during the early twentieth century women were not allowed to conduct research in university facilities. Since universities conducted most of the country's research programs, Maud found it impossible to fulfill her career goals.

With no in-country options, Maud left Canada. In Germany, Leonor Michaelis had established a research laboratory. In the fifteen years of its existence, researchers from all over the world had come to study and work with Leonor. His primary research area involved the body's chemistry—especially how it affected **enzymes** and molecules. When Maud heard about the doctor's laboratory and areas of research, she decided to go to Berlin in 1912 and study with him.

By 1912, science had already learned the basic mechanism by which enzymes work in the human body. Each enzyme turns a specific chemical compound into something else, without changing form itself or losing strength. Working together, Maud and Leonor discovered that each enzyme has its own rate of changing the chemical compound. They devised a mathematical way to measure the rate of enzyme reactions: the Michaelis-Menten equation. Researchers could now record how enzymes worked. The data obtained can be used in creating drugs to decrease the development of certain enzymes.

After working with Leonor for a year, Maud returned to the United States. She was a **research fellow** at Western Reserve University (now Case Western Reserve University) and did cancer research at the Barnard Skin and Cancer Hospital in St. Louis, Missouri. In 1916, Maud received a doctorate in biochemistry from the University of Chicago. But, even with her advanced degree, Maud could not find a university position in Canada. In 1918, Maud joined the

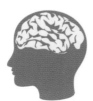

faculty of the University of Pittsburgh Medical School, where she worked until her retirement in 1950.

In 1925, Maud was promoted to assistant professor of pathology (the study of diseases, especially at the chemical level). She balanced her faculty responsibilities at the University of Pittsburgh Medical School with those as the clinical pathologist at the Children's Hospital of Pittsburgh. At Children's Hospital, Maud was responsible for surgical pathology and postmortem pathology (studying dead bodies), as well as serving as the hospital's **hematologist**.

This would have been more than enough for most people, but Maud never seemed to run out of energy. She often worked eighteen-hour days. She interacted with her students at the university, and the interns and residents at Children's Hospital often sought her out for consultations. Still, Maud made time for research and writing; over her career, she wrote or cowrote more than seventy research papers. Maud had little patience for people she felt lacked new ideas or did not work hard enough. In the article "Some Called Her Miss Menten," author Rebecca Skloot quotes Maud as commenting about a Nobel Prize-winner for medicine, "What has he done since?"

Although Maud is best known for the Michaelis-Menten equation, this was not her only discovery. Working with Helen Manning, Maud discovered in 1924 that **salmonella** raises blood glucose levels. In 1944, she, Marie Andersch, and Donald Wilson used electric charges to separate adult **hemoglobin** from fetal hemoglobin. This proved that the process—called electrophoresis—could be used to separate proteins. Although Maud and her associates used the technique first, Linus Pauling is generally credited with the discovery. Also in 1944, Maud was a member of the team that discovered the azo-dye coupling reaction. This is now used routinely in biological research and medical **diagnostics**.

In 1998, Maud was inducted into the Canadian Medical Hall of Fame. The University of Toronto also honored her, and the University of Pittsburgh established a lecture series and a chair in her memory and honor.

Despite the hours that Maud dedicated to medicine, she did take time for other activities. She loved to drive her Ford Model T. She loved to paint, and some of her paintings were exhibited with the Associated Artists of Pittsburgh. She was fluent in many languages, including Russian, French, and Italian. She played the clarinet and climbed mountains for fun.

Maud was promoted to full professor at the University of Pittsburgh in 1948; she was sixty-nine years old, one year shy of mandatory retirement. Although she had lived and worked in the United States for many years, when she retired in 1950, she returned to Canada. This time, she did not have a problem finding an institution that wanted her services. She began working for the British Columbia Medical Research Institute, conducting cancer research. In 1955, her health declining, Maud retired again. She moved to Leamington, Ontario, where she died on July 20, 1960 at the age of eight-one.

Words to Know

Monograph: a very detailed written account of a specific subject.

Enzymes: proteins produced by the cells that affect the body's metabolism.

Research fellow: a graduate student of a university who has been given a job or scholarship to conduct specialized study.

Hematologist: a doctor specializing in blood and blood-forming organs.

Salmonella: a bacteria that can cause food poisoning or typhoid fever.

Hemoglobin: the protein in red blood cells that carries oxygen throughout the body.

Diagnostics: medical procedures and tests performed to determine what is wrong with a patient.

Find Out More

Dr. Maud Menten, The Canadian Medical Hall of Fame Medi-Centre.
www.virtualmuseum.ca/Exhibitions/Medicentre/en/ment_print.htm

Proffitt, Pamela, ed. *Notable Women Scientists*. Farmington Hills, Mich.: Gale, 2000.

Skloot, Rebecca, "Some Called Her Miss Menten"
www.pittmed.health.pitt.edu/oct_2000/miss_menten.pdf

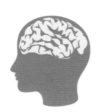

4

Gerty Theresa Cori: Nobel Prize Winner

One of the major health issues of the twenty-first century is **diabetes**. Though more is known about its causes and treatment each year, much of what is known today is based on discoveries made many years ago by a woman born in a country that no longer exists.

Gerty Theresa Radnitz was born on August 15, 1896, in Prague, which at that time was part of the Austro-Hungarian Empire. She was the oldest of three daughters born to the manager of a sugar refinery and his wife. Gerty received her early education at home from private tutors, but when she was ten years old, Gerty began attending a private girls' school.

Gerty and her husband Carl at work in their lab. Together, they won the Nobel Prize for their work on how the human body breaks down and uses sugar.

Gerty was not content with learning about how to be a "proper" young woman, the focus of education at many girls' schools of the time. She wanted more, and her uncle, a professor of **pediatrics** at the University of Prague, was her inspiration. When she graduated from the girls' school at age sixteen, Gerty knew she wanted to be a doctor. But she also knew it was not going to be an easy task. Though school had prepared her for daily life as a respectable young woman, her education had lacked coursework in subjects such as math and science. Just to get into medical school, she had to take additional classes in those subjects. She excelled and was able to enter medical school at the German University of Prague in 1914.

During medical school, Gerty decided she wanted to work in medical research, rather than treat individual patients. Another student at the medical school, Carl Cori, was also interested in research, and the two began working together. In August 1920, after both had graduated, they married and moved to Vienna.

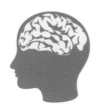

They lived and worked there until 1922, when Carl moved to Buffalo, New York, to accept a position at what was then called the State Institute for the Study of Malignant Diseases (now the Roswell Park Memorial Institute). Six months later, Gerty joined him at the institute in Buffalo.

Although the institute administrators discouraged couples from working together, it was not prohibited, and Gerty and Carl **collaborated** extensively. Their main focus was on research about how the human body produces and uses energy. They studied how the body **metabolizes** glucose and uses it for energy. The couple wrote more than fifty articles, and Gerty authored eleven articles on her own while the couple was at the institute. In 1929, the Coris published what is now called the Cori cycle, the couple's theory about how energy moves from the muscles to the liver and back to the muscles.

In 1931, the Coris moved to the Washington University School of Medicine in St. Louis, Missouri, where Carl had received a position in the Pharmacology Department. At the time, it was difficult for women to receive **prestigious** positions in medical research. Though Gerty's **credentials** were almost identical to those of her husband, she was only offered a research associate position. It took twelve years for her to be promoted to faculty status. During this time, the Coris' only child, Carl Thomas, was born.

Four years later, Gerty finally achieved full professor status. Two things happened that year—1947—that probably led to her promotion: Carl became the head of the Biochemistry Department, and the couple (along with Bernardo Houssay of Argentina) won the Nobel Prize in Physiology or Medicine for "their discovery of the course of the **catalytic** conversion of **glycogen**."

When the Coris won the Nobel Prize, Gerty became the third woman to receive the award. It was just one of many awards and honors she received during her career. Gerty's honors even extend beyond Earth. The Cori crater, located in the southern hemisphere of the moon's far side, is named after her.

In 1947, Gerty developed myelofibrosis, a bone marrow disease that affects the body's production of blood cells. She continued her lab work despite experiencing intense pain at times. On October 26, 1957, Gerty Cori died, but her achievements in the field of chemistry live on and continue to be used by chemists around the world.

Words to Know

Diabetes: usually referring to diabetes mellitus, a disorder caused by not enough insulin in the body, leading to high levels of glucose (sugar) in the blood, increased urine output, and excessive thirst.

Pediatrics: the branch of medicine concerned with caring for and treating children and babies.

Collaborated: worked together.

Metabolizes: changes through the chemical processes within the body that are necessary for life.

Prestigious: having a high status; esteemed and highly valued.

Credentials: evidence, such as a diploma or résumé, of a person's qualification to hold a particular position.

Catalytic: involving a catalyst, a substance that brings about a chemical reaction.

Glycogen: the main form of carbohydrate storage in the body; it can be easily converted to glucose by the body for energy.

Find Out More

Gerty Cori: Biography.
www.nobelprize.org/nobel_prizes/medicine/laureates/1947/cori-gt-bio.html

Women in Chemistry: Gerty Cori.
www.chemheritage.org/women_chemistry/body/cori.html

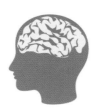

5

Hazel Bishop:
Cosmetics Chemist

What do smudge-proof lipstick and airplane engine **superchargers** have in common? Hazel Bishop. This multitalented woman is credited with both discoveries.

Hazel Bishop was born in Hoboken, New Jersey, on August 17, 1906. Her father was a very successful businessman, and she got an early education in business at the dinner table.

After Hazel graduated from high school, she attended Barnard College. She studied chemistry and planned to attend medical school when she graduated. But when she graduated with a degree in chemistry in 1929, the stock markets had just crashed and the Great Depression was beginning. Money was scarce, so, like many students at the time, Hazel got a job instead of going to medical school. She accepted a position as an assistant to **dermatologist** A. B. Cannon, who was doing research at Columbia University's College of Physicians and Surgeons. Besides researching allergies and cosmetics, Hazel took graduate-level courses in biochemistry. She eventually became the director of dermatology for the lab.

In 1942, as World War II raged, Hazel left Columbia to work for the Standard Oil Company. There, she worked to discover the causes of deposits that were affecting the superchargers of airplane engines. After the end of World War II, she moved to Mobil Oil, where she worked on **formulations** for different types of gasoline.

Gasoline was not Hazel's only project, however. After work, she would go home and work some more in her kitchen. Sometimes she cooked food, but she also used her kitchen as a lab. Hazel was trying to discover a new lipstick. Many women loved wearing lipstick, but they were not happy about having to reapply it several times a day. When their lips touched something, they left a lip imprint behind. Hazel wanted to use her knowledge of chemistry to develop a lipstick that would not leave those telltale lip prints on glasses and cups, eating utensils, clothing, and other people. She also wanted it to be nonirritating and nondrying

What is an Assistantship?

Many colleges and universities help graduate students by giving assistantships. If you get an assistantship, you will usually help professors with their responsibilities as either teaching assistants or research assistants. Rather than receive hourly wages, students often get a stipend that offsets some or all of their tuition. Assistantships provide much needed experience for graduate students, increasing their future employment options.

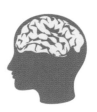

A 1952 advertisement for Hazel's lipstick.

to the wearer's lips. In 1949, she hit on a solution. Instead of simply coating lips with a color, as the lipsticks of the time did, Hazel discovered that if the lipstick contained colorants called bromo acids, the lips would be stained, not simply covered. This meant the lipstick would last a long time—and stay on the wearer's lips.

The following year, Hazel joined Raymond Spector, an advertising man, to form Hazel Bishop Cosmetics Inc. to produce and sell her product. Her lipstick was an instant success. In the summer of 1950, the department store Lord & Taylor added the lipstick—it cost $1 per tube—to its cosmetics counter. It sold out in

one day. Before long, Hazel's groundbreaking lipstick controlled one-quarter of the lipstick market, going up against major cosmetic companies like Revlon.

As Hazel's discovery became increasingly successful, so did her company's profits. By 1953, the company was earning $10 million per year. Her original investor and business partner, Raymond Spector, wanted more control and more of the company profits. He bought up the majority of the company's shares and managed to push Hazel out of her own company.

Hazel did not wallow in self-pity about the loss of her company. Instead, she established Hazel Bishop Laboratories in 1954. Now, along with lipstick, Hazel also worked to develop household and personal-care products. One of her most successful products was Leather Lav, a glove cleaner. Once again, Spector entered the picture, launching a successful lawsuit to stop Hazel from selling the products under her own name.

By the early 1960s, Hazel had left the cosmetic industry. In 1962, she began her career in finance, first as a stockbroker with Bache & Company, and then as a financial analyst with Evans & Company. As the cosmetic industry grew during the 1960s and 1970s, Hazel's expertise was highly sought out by companies and the financial media. Before they launched a new product, many companies wanted her opinion about its likelihood of success. When a financial publication or broker wanted to know the same thing, it was Hazel whom they trusted for honest—and accurate—information. She became the "go-to" person when anyone wanted information and opinions about industry trends.

In 1978, Hazel took a position as a professor at the Fashion Institute of Technology in New York City. She taught in a program for students preparing for careers in the cosmetic field. In 1980, Hazel was appointed to the Revlon Chair in Cosmetics Marketing at the institute, named after her former competitor.

After leaving the industry, Hazel continued to create lipstick—but now it was just for her. Her signature shade was red, with just a hint of blue.

Even though the name Hazel Bishop is usually connected with lipstick and the cosmetics industry, she was first and foremost a chemist. Her colleagues recognized her importance to the field of chemistry, and in 1971, she became the first female member of The Chemists' Club, an important professional organization in New York City.

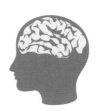

Hazel Bishop, inventor and **innovator**, died at the age of ninety-two in 1998 in Rye, New York. Throughout her life, she had used chemistry to do amazing things.

Words to Know

Superchargers: blowers used to supply air under high pressure to the cylinders of an internal combustion engine.

Dermatologist: a doctor who specializes in treating skin conditions.

Formulations: substances prepared according to specific combinations of chemicals.

Innovator: a pioneer in a new field; someone who helps develop new directions in research, technology, or art.

Find Out More

Bishop, Hazel, 1906–1998, Papers ca. 1890–1998: A Finding Aid
www.oasis.lib.harvard.edu/oasis/deliver/~sch00355

Inventor of the Week
www.web.mit.edu/invent/iow/bishop.html

Women in Chemistry: Hazel Bishop
www.chemheritage.org/women_chemistry/style/bishop.html

6

Dorothy Crowfoot Hodgkin:
Social Activist & Chemist

Imagine trying to pick up a grain of salt. Now imagine trying to do it with hands that are gnarled with arthritis. Though it was difficult, and sometimes painful, Dorothy Crowfoot Hodgkin did not let arthritis stop her from mounting and photographing the salt-sized crystals that she needed for her research.

Dorothy Mary Crowfoot was born in Cairo, Egypt, on May 12, 1910. Her parents, John and Molly, were British colonial administrators and archaeologists in North Africa and the Middle East. Her parents sent her and her three sisters to England to go to school. The girls attended a coed, public secondary school in Beccles, Suffolk.

Like many schools, certain classes were not open to girls. When Dorothy learned that girls were not allowed to study science at her school, she was not satisfied to settle for taking a subject someone else had decided was more "acceptable" for girls. Dorothy was determined that she be allowed into the all-boys science classes. She had developed a fascination with crystals when she was ten years old, and she wanted the opportunity to study them. Dorothy's determination paid off, and she was allowed to take the science classes she wanted.

In 1928, Dorothy was admitted to Somerville College at the University of Oxford, where she studied chemistry. During her first year, Dorothy combined the study of archaeology and chemistry, but after a class in **crystallography**, she decided to concentrate in X-ray crystallography. Before Conrad Roentgen discovered X-rays in 1895, those who studied crystals had surmised that they were made of an orderly arrangement of atoms. They could hypothesize something about this orderliness by taking measurements of the angles between crystal faces. With the discovery of X-rays, scientists had a way to see inside crystals and make a detailed determination of crystal structures and cell size. In one of the highlights of her undergraduate work, Dorothy became one of the first to study the structure of an organic compound by using X-ray crystallography.

After graduating from Somerville College in 1932, Dorothy enrolled at the University of Cambridge to pursue her doctorate. She also wanted the opportunity to work with physicist John Desmond Bernal, who was a pioneer in X-ray crystallography. Dorothy took advantage of the opportunities she had working in his laboratory. She took the work he had completed on biological molecules and added to it. Dorothy helped him use X-ray crystallography to study the protein pepsin, an enzyme that aids digestion.

In 1934, Dorothy returned to Somerville and Oxford, where she remained until she retired. Almost immediately on her arrival, she began fund-raising to buy some X-ray equipment. With the help of her efforts and foundation contributions, she was able to purchase much-needed equipment. Dorothy set up an X-ray laboratory at the Oxford University Museum of Natural History. Instead of X-raying dinosaur bones, however, she spent much of her time taking X-rays of insulin, a hormone secreted by cells within the pancreas. She was using X-rays to study chemistry!

In 1937, Dorothy married historian Thomas Hodgkin. The following year, she gave birth to the couple's first child. Shortly after the baby's birth, Dorothy contracted an infection. As a result, she developed chronic rheumatoid arthritis, which left her hands swollen and malformed. Placing small crystals on mounting slides and photographing them became difficult, but Dorothy continued with her work.

Dorothy put her insulin research on the backburner in 1939. Fellow Oxford researcher Howard Florey had isolated penicillin, and he wanted Dorothy and her group to determine its chemical makeup. It took six years, but in 1945, she succeeded. Penicillin became, at that time, the largest molecule to have its structure determined through X-ray crystallography. Dorothy's success also ended a dispute in the scientific community about penicillin's makeup. In 1947, in acknowledgment of Dorothy's discovery, she became only the second woman elected to the Royal Society, the preeminent scientific organization in Britain.

During the mid-1950s, Dorothy turned her research attention to vitamin B12. This vitamin helps maintain healthy blood and nerve cells. It is normally involved in the **metabolism** of every cell of the body, especially those affecting DNA (the molecules that control heredity), but also in fatty acid synthesis and energy production. This time, Dorothy had more than X-ray crystallography to aid her in her chemical research. She used a computer to do the complex computations necessary to her findings.

Dorothy's work with penicillin brought her more **accolades**. In 1960, she became the first Wolfson Research Professor of the Royal Society. In 1964, she won the Nobel Prize for Chemistry, "for her determinations by X-ray techniques of the structures of important biochemical substances."

Though her study of insulin was often put aside for other projects, Dorothy never forgot about it. The complex makeup of the large molecule could not be determined until the tools used to analyze it got bigger and better. Finally, in 1969, Dorothy and her team of researchers were able to use improved X-ray crystallography techniques and a much faster computer to finally crack the chemical mystery of insulin structure.

Dorothy was also involved in the larger scientific community. In 1946, she participated in the meetings that eventually led to the founding of the International

Union of Crystallography. She traveled to scientific conferences and conducted research in many countries, including China and the United States.

Like many scientists, Dorothy was a social activist. After her retirement from Somerville, Oxford in 1977, she spent much of her time supporting the cause of scientists in developing countries. She was especially concerned about those in China and India. From 1975 to 1988, Dorothy was president of the Pugwash Conferences on Science and World Affairs. The conferences bring together scientists from all over the world to discuss the peaceful means of achieving international security development and how science can help accomplish those goals.

Eventually, Dorothy's rheumatoid arthritis made it impossible for her to maintain such a busy schedule. She died at the age of eighty-four on July 29, 1994, in Shipston-on-Stour, Warwickshire, England. Her life has made a difference to our world today, because she used her knowledge of chemistry to solve important medical problems

Words to Know

Crystallography: the study of the formation and structure of crystals.
Metabolism: the chemical processes occurring within the body that are necessary to maintain life.
Accolades: expressions of praise, approval, and acknowledgment.

Find Out More

Biography: Dorothy Crowfoot Hodgkin
www.nobelprize.org/nobel_prizes/chemistry/laureates/1964/hodgkin-bio.html

Dorothy Crowfoot Hodgkin, OM
www.sdsc.edu/ScienceWomen/hodgkin.html

Ferry, Georgina. *Dorothy Hodgkin: A Life.* Woodbury, N.Y.: Cold Spring Harbor Laboratory Press, 2000.

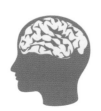

7

Marie Maynard Daly:
Connections Between Diet & Health

In the 1940s, it was rare for an African American man to earn an advanced degree in chemistry. And for African American women, it was impossible—at least until Marie Maynard Daly came along.

Marie Maynard Daly was born in Corona, Queens, New York, on April 16, 1921. Her father, Ivan, who was originally from the British West Indies, had attended Cornell University in Ithaca, New York, for a semester. Ivan wanted to become a chemist. Although he had a scholarship, he and his family could not afford the room and board, and he was forced to drop out. Though Ivan was un-

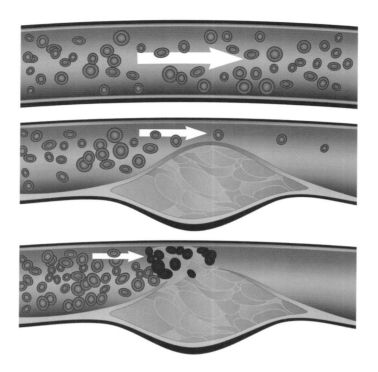

Because of Marie's research, people today understand the connection between too much cholesterol in the diet and various health problems. As shown here, when cholesterol builds up inside the blood vessels, it gets in the way of blood flow. This can cause high blood pressure, heart disease, and other serious health issues.

able to earn his college degree (he became a postal clerk instead), he and his wife Helen instilled the importance of education in their children.

Marie attended Hunter College High School, a prestigious all-girl school in Manhattan. Like her father, Marie wanted to become a chemist. The school's teachers encouraged her to pursue her dreams, and she was able to take classes that prepared her for future studies in the science field.

After graduating from Hunter College High School, Marie attended Queens College in Flushing, New York. She was able to live at home and save the money that would have been spent on room and board had she attended a college or university further from home. In 1942, Marie graduated **magna cum laude** from Queens College with a degree in chemistry. She was also named a Queens College Scholar in recognition of her academic achievements and was inducted into the Phi Beta Kappa and Sigma Xi honor societies.

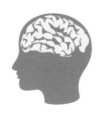

Marie taught at Queens College while attending graduate school at New York University. A year later, she earned a master's degree and enrolled in the doctoral program at Columbia University. While in the doctoral program, Marie worked under the guidance of Mary L. Caldwell and began to research enzymes and digestion, an area she would be involved in throughout her career. Marie was awarded her doctorate from New York University in 1947, becoming the first African American woman in the United States to receive a doctorate in chemistry.

After graduation, Marie accepted a teaching position at Howard University in Washington, D.C., where she taught physical science. In 1951, she received a grant from the American Cancer Society for postgraduate study and research. Marie returned to New York and worked closely with molecular biologist Alfred Mirsky at the Rockefeller Institute. By 1955, Marie had moved on to teach biochemistry at the College of Physicians and Surgeons of Columbia University. While there, Marie had the opportunity to work with Quentin Demming, who was researching the causes of heart attacks. She and Demming left Columbia in 1960 to go to Albert Einstein College of Medicine at Yeshiva University in New York City, where Marie was appointed to a professorship, and where she worked until her retirement in 1986. In 1961, she married Vincent Clark.

Besides her interest in metabolism, Marie also researched cholesterol's effects on the **cardiac** system, the effects of **nutrients**—especially various forms of sugar—on the arteries, and the effects of advanced age and high blood pressure on the body's circulatory system. Today, the connection between heart health and cholesterol, lipids, and fats is well known and accepted. Marie's work helped advance medical science's understanding of cardiac health, thereby leading to the development of **preventive care** as well as methods of treating heart conditions.

Though Marie spent most of her career as a teacher, she also had other medical-related positions. From 1958 until 1963, she was an investigator for the American Heart Association. Between 1962 and 1972, she was a career scientist for the Health Research Council of New York. She was also a fellow of the Council on Arteriosclerosis and the American Association for the Advancement of Science. From 1974 to 1976, she was a member of the New York Academy of Science.

Marie's associations extended beyond the scientific community. She was very aware of her position as a role model for other African Americans. She symbolized what individuals could achieve through hard work and determination. Marie was involved with the NAACP (National Association for the Advancement of Colored People) and the National Association of Negro Business and Professional Women. She wanted to encourage minority students to enroll in medical and other science-related graduate programs. In 1988, Marie established a scholarship fund for African American chemistry and physics students at Queens College in memory of her father.

Marie Maynard Daly died on October 28, 2003. Throughout her lifetime, she had used chemistry to improve the world's understanding of the connections between the food we eat and our health. Because of her, we can all live healthier lives!

Words to Know

Magna cum laude: "with great praise," a Latin phrase used to indicate high academic achievement on a graduation diploma.

Cardiac: having to do with the heart.

Nutrients: the substances in food that are necessary for life and maintaining health.

Preventive care: medical care intended to keep people healthy and prevent diseases, rather than treat already-existing illnesses.

Find Out More

Clark, Marie Maynard Daly
www.blackpast.org/?q=aah/clark-marie-maynard-daly-1921-2003

Marie Maynard Daly
www.aaregistry.com/detail.php?id=2448

Warren, Wini. *Black Women Scientists in the United States*. Bloomington: Indiana University Press, 2000.

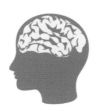

8

Helen Murray Free
Chemisty & Diabetes

Having diabetes is not easy. Watching one's diet and keeping track of blood-glucose levels can be complicated and disruptive to daily activities. But as difficult as it can be, it would be much harder without the contribution of Helen Murray Free.

Helen Murray was born in 1923 in Pittsburgh, Pennsylvania, where her father James worked for a coal company. Her mother Daisy had died of influenza when Helen was six years old.

In 1941, Helen was valedictorian of her graduating class at Seminary High School in Poland, Ohio. She enrolled at the College of Wooster in Wooster, Ohio, with the intention of majoring in English and becoming a teacher. When the Japanese attacked Pearl Harbor on December 7, 1941, and the United States entered World War II, Helen changed her mind about a major. As U.S. involvement in the war intensified, women were needed to fill factory jobs left empty as young men were called to fight. When Helen's dorm mother suggested that some of the girls should take up science so they could replace the men who had gone off to war, Helen was up to the challenge. She was on her way to a career that would help millions.

Helen proved to be very good in chemistry. But despite her academic achievements, she was not exactly swamped with job offers as she prepared for graduation—she received only one offer. She was not anxious to accept a job testing creosote on fence posts, so instead she applied for a research fellowship at the Mellon Institute in Pittsburgh, Pennsylvania. In the meantime, a former professor set up an interview for her with Miles Laboratories, Inc. (today part of Bayer AG). Despite what she felt was a lukewarm response from her male interviewers, Helen was offered a position as a control chemist in the laboratory. Though it was not what she really wanted to do—she wanted to do research— Helen accepted the position. She had not heard from Mellon about the fellowship, and she needed a job. After graduation in 1944 with a Bachelor of Science degree in chemistry, Helen moved to Indiana and began what would be a thirty-year career with Miles.

Helen did finally hear from Mellon a few weeks after taking the position with Miles. They had awarded her the fellowship. But since Helen had made a commitment to Miles, she turned it down.

It did not take long before Helen tired of being a control chemist, though. When she learned there would be an opening in the research division, she applied and was hired by the new biochemist, Alfred Free. Alfred and Helen worked well together, both inside and outside the laboratory. They soon became a couple and married in 1947. They would have six children.

From the beginning, diabetes treatment was one of the couple's primary research responsibilities. When the Frees began their work, Miles already had a urine test on the market to determine blood-glucose levels, but they wanted a more accurate test. The Frees created a test that was more accurate and made

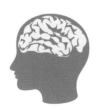

Why Was the Frees' Work So Important?

If a person has hyperglycemia—a high blood-glucose level—long-term damage can be done to the body's organs. Kidney and heart disease and vision problems can develop, for example. This is why it's so important that someone with diabetes keep track of his insulin levels. If the readings remain high for a period of time, an increased insulin dose may be required. If the blood-glucose level is too low, death can occur. Relying on symptoms alone is not a reliable method of measuring blood-glucose levels. Fatigue, increased intake of fluids, and frequent urination—all symptoms of high glucose levels—have other causes as well. Low blood-glucose levels require immediate attention because of the possibility of death. Trembling, anxiety, sweating, headaches, and extreme hunger are not reliable indicators of low blood glucose levels, however. Only monitoring can indicate whether a regular dose of insulin could lead to a crisis situation.

it easier to test blood-glucose levels. All a doctor, nurse, or technician had to do was place a tablet in a test tube and add a solution containing the urine to be tested. The amount of color change would determine the blood-glucose level. Now, instead of going to a hospital to have the test done, blood-glucose levels could be checked in the doctor's office. Eventually, patients were able to do the tests themselves at home.

Helen and her husband then went to work on an even easier way to test urine for blood-glucose levels. They and their research team developed a paper "dipstick" for testing. The paper was coated with chemicals that changed color when dipped in a urine sample. The color would indicate the blood-glucose level. Making it easier to test blood-glucose levels made it more likely that people with

In an interview, Helen describes how she first became interested in chemistry: "In September 1941, I was going to the College of Wooster to be a Latin and English teacher. Then Pearl Harbor happened in December, and the fellas all left to join the Navy and the Air Force. One night, the house mother came in and said, 'Helen, you're taking chemistry and getting good grades … why don't you switch?' And I just said OK. I fell in love with chemistry, and it was wonderful."

diabetes would perform this important test. Potentially dangerous situations could be avoided with an accurate method of measuring blood-glucose levels.

Although Helen's research focused on diabetes treatment, she also found ways to use some of the same techniques to test for other health issues. For example, Helen's team took the idea of using a tablet to test for the presence of a substance and created one to test for hepatitis A (a serious liver disease). When a urine sample came in contact with the tablet, it would change colors if the urine contained bilirubin (the orange-yellow substance found in the liver), which

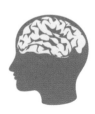

meant the individual might have hepatitis A. Helen's team also expanded on their diagnostic test strips and developed one that tested for ten things on one strip.

The Frees received seven **patents** for their diagnostic test inventions. Both Frees were inducted into the National Inventors Hall of Fame in 2000.

Helen didn't restrict herself to the laboratory. In 1978, she received a master's degree in management, with an emphasis in health-care administration, from Central Michigan University. She taught management at Indiana University for almost twenty years. She has also been active in the American Chemistry Society, and an award for public outreach is named in her honor. In 1980, Helen received that organization's Garvan Medal, which recognizes outstanding achievement by a woman.

Since her retirement, she has spent much of her time educating people about how chemistry impacts their lives. And people with diabetes can thank Helen for being able to live with their disease far more safely.

Words to Know

Patents: the rights to make, sell, and use a particular invention for a particular period of time, often given to the inventor by a government.

Find Out More

Hall of Fame/Inventor Profile
www.invent.org/Hall_Of_Fame/63

Helen Murray Free
www.nsdl.org/resource/2200/20061121124407862T

Inventor of the Week Archive: Helen Murray Free
www.mit.edu/invent/iow/free.html

Vare, Ethlie, and Greg Ptacek. *Patently Female: From AZT to TV Dinners, Stories of Women Inventors and Their Breakthrough Ideas*. New York: Wiley, 2002.

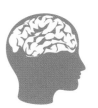

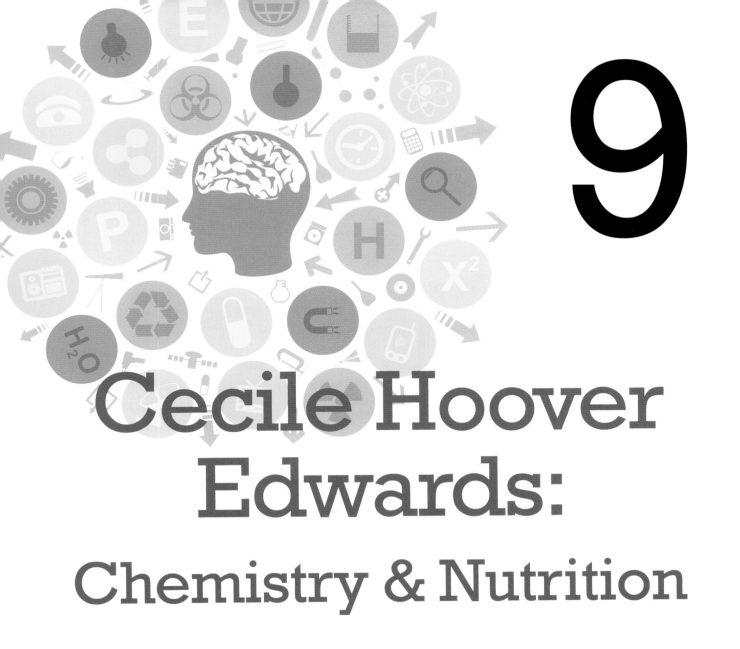

9

Cecile Hoover Edwards:
Chemistry & Nutrition

L ike George Washington Carver, who did groundbreaking work with peanuts, Cecile Hoover Edwards was an African American scientist who worked in food and nutrition. Cecile Hoover Edwards' chemistry knowledge improved the health and lives of countless people.

Cecile Annette Hoover was born in 1926 in East Saint Louis, Illinois, the third of five children. An excellent student, Cecile graduated from high school when she was fifteen years old. Her mother encouraged her to attend the Tuskegee Institute (today known as Tuskegee University) in Alabama.

Today, chemists use machines like this one to analyze amino acids. Researchers are still discovering more connections between these chemicals and human health.

Cecile continued to exhibit her outstanding academic abilities at Tuskegee. She graduated with high honors in 1946 with a bachelor's degree in home economics and a double minor in nutrition and chemistry. She earned a master's degree in chemistry at Tuskegee in 1947. Cecile's academic record led to a General Education Board Fellowship that allowed her to continue her education at Iowa State University in Ames.

At Iowa State University, Cecile worked on a doctorate in nutrition. She also studied **physiological chemistry** and **microscopic anatomy**. Though Cecile completed her doctoral requirements in two years, a member of the doctoral committee did not think she was old enough, at twenty-two, to graduate. The other committee members were convinced, and Cecile continued her research. When she was finally granted her doctorate, her **dissertation** was more than 400 pages of high-quality research and conclusions.

Cecile accepted a position on the faculty of Tuskegee in 1950. In April 1951, Cecile met Gerald A. Edwards at North Carolina A&T College in Greensboro, where both presented papers at the National Institute of Science's annual meeting. They married two months later. Both Cecile and Gerald worked at Tuskegee until 1956, when they were awarded a research grant from the National

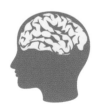

Institutes of Health. They—and their grant—moved to A&T, where they researched the metabolism of an **amino acid** called methionine in rats.

In 1966, Cecile and her family, which now included children, moved to India for two years. She and Gerald continued researching amino acids and also investigated nutrition in India.

The Edwards family then moved to Washington, D.C. in early 1971, and Cecile became a professor of nutrition in the Department of Home Economics at Howard University. In the fall, she became the chairwoman of the department. One of her first tasks was to design the curriculum for the School of Human Ecology. Cecile was dean of the school from 1974 until 1986. She put into place the doctoral program in nutrition, making Howard University the only predominately African American college with such a program. Cecile stayed at the school until she retired in 2000.

Throughout her career, Cecile studied amino acids, which the body uses to create the protein necessary for good health. Cecile wanted everyone, including minorities and those who were economically disadvantaged, to have the best nutrition available and at the lowest cost possible. She wanted to find a combination of less-expensive foods that, when eaten together, would lead to the body's greatest production of protein. Cecile felt this was best accomplished when the bulk of the diet consisted of vegetables rather than meat.

She was also concerned about the amount of fat that characterized the diets of many minorities, especially those of African Americans raised in the South. Otherwise healthy foods such as greens and beans were often cooked with ham hocks or other fatty pork products used as seasonings. Chicken and fish, generally much lower in fat than beef, were frequently cooked in lard, which turned them from a relatively healthy food to a high-fat, high-cholesterol food. Cecile knew that it was not practical to expect people to give up their beloved dishes. Instead, she worked on ways to reduce the amount of fat contained in favorite dishes.

Cecile was also concerned about the role diet played in pregnancy. For many years, Cecile researched how poor diet affected an unborn child. Her results led to a better understanding of the relationship between pregnancy and nutrition.

Cecile did not limit her concerns for minorities and the disadvantaged to nutrition. In 1969, Arthur Jensen, then a professor of educational psychology

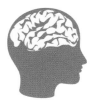

at the University of California, Berkeley, published an article claiming that a significant proportion of one's IQ was **predetermined** by race. Many people interpreted this to mean that minorities were **inherently** less intelligent. In 1992, Cecile brought together nutritionists, biochemists, psychologists, sociologists, and other scientists to research Jensen's claim. The National Institutes of Health gave the group a grant to aid in and publish its research that proved that Jensen's claim was wrong.

Cecile Edwards received many awards and acknowledgments for her work. After a life filled with accomplishments, awards, and recognition, and the knowledge that she had made a difference, Cecile Hoover Edwards died in 2005. Her knowledge of chemistry had contributed to a world where people now better understand the connections between diet and health.

Words to Know

Physiological chemistry: chemical studies relating to the normal functioning of an organism.
Microscopic anatomy: the study of the structures of living things that cannot be seen with the naked eye.
Dissertation: a long, in-depth research paper written to complete a PhD program.
Amino acid: an organic compound used as the building blocks of proteins and as a chemical messenger.
Predetermined: decided in advance.
Inherently: having to do with the person's most basic nature.

Find Out More

Cecile Hoover Edwards
www.chemheritage.org/women_chemistry/food/edwards.html

Warren, Wini. *Black Women Scientists in the United States*. Bloomington: Indiana University Press, 2000.

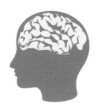

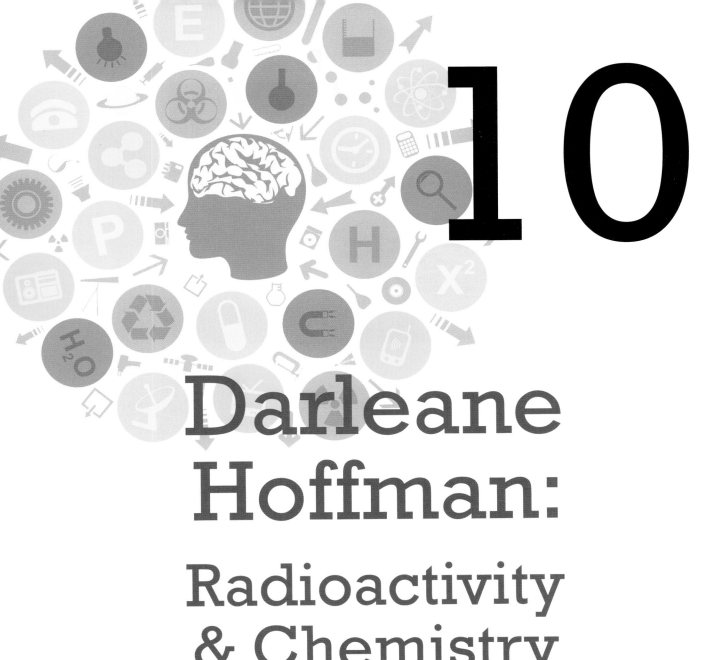

10

Darleane Hoffman:

Radioactivity & Chemistry

Many people chase **elusive** dreams, but Darleane Hoffman chases something even more elusive. Among her quests are some of the universe's rarest elements.

Darleane Christian was born on November 8, 1926, in Terril, a very small, rural town in northwest Iowa. After she graduated from high school, Darleane enrolled in what was then called Iowa State College (now Iowa State University), with a major in applied art. To fulfill one of her major's requirements, Darleane

Darleane received the National Medal of Science from President Bill Clinton in 1997.

took a beginning chemistry class during the spring 1945 semester. Inspired by her professor, Dr. Nellie Naylor, Darleane changed her major to physical chemistry.

But it was not a decision that came easily. She was certain she wanted a career in science, but having a family was also important to her. In those days, it was hard enough for a woman to build a career as a scientist, without trying to have a family as well. Dr. Naylor had remained single, but Darleane was reluctant to take the same path. For inspiration, she turned to the story of Marie Curie, who had an incredibly successful career and raised two children. If Marie could do it, Darleane was sure she could as well.

During Darleane's junior year, she got a research assistant's position at the university's Institute of Atomic Research. Her first job at the institute was to build Geiger counters, which are used to detect radiation and other particles.

After graduation, Darleanne stayed at Iowa State to earn her doctorate. She also met and married another graduate student, Marvin Hoffman; the couple eventually had two children. With her doctorate in hand, Darleane moved to Ten-

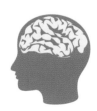

nessee to take a job at Oak Ridge National Laboratory; Marvin joined her after he completed his course requirements. Los Alamos National Laboratory hired Marvin after he received his doctorate in 1952, and the couple moved to New Mexico.

On November 1, 1952, "Mike"—the code name given to the first test of a multi-megaton thermonuclear weapon—exploded on Enewetak Atoll, 2,500 miles southwest of Hawaii. In the debris left behind by the test, scientists found einsteinium and fermium. Sitting on the sidelines because her security clearance had not yet arrived, Darleane was frustrated because she could not participate in the chemical research.

Darleane began work at Oak Ridge in 1953, as soon as she had her security clearance. One of the elements that had been found in Mike's debris was plutonium-244. Plutonium is a rare, **radioactive**, metallic, chemical element; 244 is the isotope number, a particular version of plutonium. Darleane began looking for the element within the Earth's crust. After a search that lasted for two years, Darleane and her colleagues became the first people to find the elusive 244 isotope within a rock formation that dated back to Precambrian time. Before Darleane's discovery, it was believed that heavy metals (those with atomic numbers higher than 92, the atomic number of uranium, previously believed to be the "heaviest" metal) did not occur naturally. Darleane proved that was not the case.

Darleane has also done extensive work in the chemistry of heavy metals. Through her work, she discovered another characteristic of these elements: they disintegrate rapidly. Hahnium (also known as dubnium) has a half-life of only thirty-five seconds. This means that in thirty-five seconds, the element has lost half of its radioactivity through decay. To be able to study the chemical makeup of short-lived elements, Darleane and her colleagues developed the "one-atom-at-a-time" technique. This method calls for researchers to measure the rate of decay of individual atoms, combine results, and compare them to other known elements.

During the 1970s, Darleane researched properties of nuclear fission. In the fission process, an atom's nucleus is split. Since nuclear fission's discovery in the 1930s, it was believed that the only way to cause the nucleus to split was to

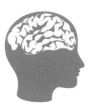

hit it with a bombardment of neutrons. Darleane found, however, that the element fermium's atoms could split on their own, without any outside influence.

In 1984, Darleane left Oak Ridge to take a professorship in chemistry at the University of California, Berkeley, and an appointment as a chemist in the Nuclear Science Division at the U.S. Department of Energy's Lawrence Berkeley National Laboratory (Berkeley Lab). Her work at the lab would allow her to continue her search for "superheavy" elements, those elements that would decay almost immediately.

In 1999, Darleane was part of a group at the Berkeley Lab that announced the discovery of two superheavy elements: Element 118 and Element 116, the result of Element 118's decay. One of the criteria for acceptable scientific research is the ability to replicate results. In other words, the findings can't be a "one-shot deal"; they can be repeated. Two years later, the group had to take back their findings—therefore their discovery—because they believed the results could not be repeated; one of the researchers had fabricated his part of the results. In 2006, however, a group of Russian and American scientists reported that they had discovered Element 118.

Darleane has served on many government advisory boards, including the National Research Council's Committee on Nuclear and Radiochemistry. She is also concerned about the safety of nuclear waste and has served on the National Academy of Science's Board on Radioactive Waste and the National Research Council's Board of Radioactive Waste Management.

Darleane is a member of many chemical societies, and she has won many awards. Her career in chemistry allows here to take part in one of the most important issues of our day—the dangers of nuclear waste. Her work will help build a safer world for us all.

Words to Know

Elusive: difficult to grasp or capture.
Radioactive: the property of an atomic nucleus that results in an emission of energy via photons or tiny subatomic particles.

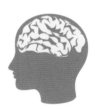

Find Out More

Darleane Hoffman
www.chemheritage.org/women_chemistry/univ/hoffman.html

Research News
www.lbl.gov/Science-Articles/Archive/elements-116-118.html

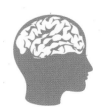

11
Opportunities for Women in Chemistry Today

These pioneering women broke ground for the new generations of women who are becoming chemists today. Today, lots of people realize that more women should be given the chance to be chemists. As more opportunities open up, more women are choosing careers in chemistry.

Growing Trends

Many programs work to get more women interested in science, technology, engineering, and math (STEM) classes and careers. As a result, more women are joining these fields. Chemistry is one of the sciences that attracts the most women. In high school and college, the same number of girls and boys take chemistry. Numbers of women drop, though, in graduate education. A smaller percentage of women make up Ph.D. graduates. And fewer still end up becoming professors or working at high levels at companies.

However, more and more women are getting Ph.D.s and are becoming professors. It wasn't too long ago that almost no women were doing those things. It's taking time, and while some people are frustrated with the slow progress, women are becoming a more important part of chemistry every year.

There are now labs headed by women. There are labs that are made up entirely of women. It's not unusual to see women in lab coats, testing important hypotheses. Nor is it strange to see a women teaching chemistry to college students. Women are here to stay in the field of chemistry.

How Much Does a Career in Chemistry Earn?

The average yearly wages of chemists were $71,070 in May 2008. Materials scientists had average yearly wages of $81,600. According to the National Association of Colleges and Employers, beginning salary offers in July 2009 for graduates with a bachelor's degree in chemistry averaged $39,897 a year. In March 2009, yearly earnings of chemists in the federal government averaged $101,687.

Continuing Challenges

Women have made a lot of progress in chemistry these days. However, there are still plenty of challenges left.

Some people may still be **biased** against women in science, even if they don't say they are. Sometimes people don't even know they treat female scientists

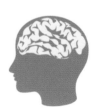

differently, even though there is evidence that they do. For example, a recent report found that science professors were more likely to give male students better opportunities. It didn't matter if female chemists were equally qualified.

Researchers asked a group of science professors to take a look at a job application a "student" had made for a lab manager position. (The application wasn't real.) Half the applications had the name John on them, and the other half had the name Jennifer. Otherwise, they were exactly the same. The researchers found that both male and female professors were less likely to offer the female applicant the job. And when they did offer her the job, she was given a lower salary. Probably none of those professors would have said they were **sexist**. But their actions showed they were biased against women!

Although most people would say that women are an important part of science today, problems still exist. Female chemists often make less money, and

How Many Jobs Are There?

Chemists and materials scientists held about 94,100 jobs in 2008. About 4 out of 10 jobs were in manufacturing firms. A lot of the firms were in the chemical manufacturing industry. This industry produces plastics and synthetic materials, drugs, soaps and cleaners, paints, industrial organic chemicals, and other chemical products.

The Future of Chemistry

There will be job openings in industries that sell things that a lot of people need or want to buy, like medicine. In other industries, it will be harder for a chemist to get a job, especially when the economy is not doing well. Employers are especially looking for chemists and materials scientists who have a master's or Ph.D. degree. Those with only a bachelor's degree might find a job as a research assistant.

they have to fight unconscious biases against them. Still there are growing opportunities for women in this field today.

Although a career in chemistry is not always easy, the women who forged ahead in the past have made it a little easier and a little fairer for the women in chemistry today. We can thank them, and female chemists today, for continuing to make science a more equal place for all genders.

Words to Know

Biased: to show unfair favor for or against an individual or group.
Sexist: belief that one sex (male or female) is better than the other, or is more or less valuable; sexism also includes actions based on those beliefs.

Find Out More

Balbes, LIsa. *Nontraditional Careers for Chemists: New Formulas in Chemistry*. New York: Oxford University Press,

Ferguson. *Careers in Focus: Chemistry*. New York: Facts on File, 2008.

Franceschetti, Donald. *Careers in Chemistry*. Ipswich, Mass.: Salem Press, 2013.

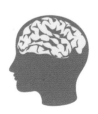

Index

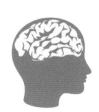

About the Author & Consultant

Kim Etingoff lives in Boston, Massachusetts, spending part of her time working on farms. Kim has written a number of books for young people on topics including health, history, nutrition, and business.

Ann Lee-Karlon, PhD, is the President of the Association for Women in Science (AWIS) in 2014–2016. AWIS is a national nonprofit organization dedicated to advancing women in science, technology, engineering, and mathematics. Dr. Lee-Karlon also serves as Senior Vice President at Genentech, a major biotechnology company focused on discovering and developing medicines for serious diseases such as cancer. Dr. Lee-Karlon holds a BS in Bioengineering from the University of California at Berkeley, an MBA from Stanford University, and a PhD in Bioengineering from the University of California at San Diego, where she was a National Science Foundation Graduate Research Fellow. She completed a postdoctoral fellowship at the University College London as an NSF International Research Fellow. Dr. Lee-Karlon holds several U.S. and international patents in vascular and tissue engineering.

Picture Credits

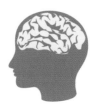